The Black Snowman

by *Phil Mendez*

Illustrated by Carole Byard

SCHOLASTIC INC. • *New York*

Text copyright © 1989 by Phil Mendez.

Illustrations copyright © 1989 by Carole Byard.

All rights reserved. Published by Scholastic Inc.

SCHOLASTIC HARDCOVER is a registered trademark of Scholastic Inc.

Library of Congress Cataloging-in-Publication Data

Mendez, Phil.
The black snowman.

Summary: Through the powers of a magical *kente*
a black snowman comes to life and helps young Jacob
discover the beauty of his black heritage as well
as his own self-worth.
[1. Afro-Americans—Fiction. 2. Snowmen—Fiction.
3. Self-acceptance—Fiction] I. Byard, Carole, ill.
II. Title.
PZ7.M52535B1   1989   [E]   87-4774
ISBN 0-590-40552-7

12 11 10 9 8 7 6 5 4 3 2   9/8 0 1 2 3 4/9
Printed in the U.S.A.   36

First Scholastic printing, October 1989

Designed by Claire Counihan

To Fred and Caroline Kotkov.
—P.M.

For my children, Michael, Keith, Nasheet,
Kijana, Ayodele, Kwame, and Sienna.
Listen to the drum within
and be all that you are.
—C.B.

Somewhere in a lonely grass hut in western Africa, an aged storyteller prepares for the arrival of the village children. He tells stories of Anansi the spider: stories of how Anansi's head came to be so small and of how jealousy came to the Ashanti tribe.

The storyteller is ready, except for one important thing: a brightly colored kente. As he wraps the cloth around him, his mind transforms into that of a young native. As an old man, he has forgotten the many stories; but when he wears his magic kente, the stories are quick and sharp in his mind. The kente restores his memory.

The storytelling ritual continues for many years. Village children grow up, have their own children, and send them to hear and to learn. But one day the storytelling comes to an end.

Invaders capture the villagers and seize their property. The prisoners are loaded onto ships that cross a vast ocean to the continent called America, where the African people are sold into slavery.

The magic kente is sold, too. It passes through generations, even after slavery is no more. A thousand uses fray its delicate threads until it is discarded as a useless rag. But it still possesses the magic . . . it still has wonders to perform.

Jacob Miller always woke up late on Saturday mornings. But not today. When his eyes opened, his heart was beating rapidly. He did not remember his dream, but it must have been a bad one. He felt frightened. He felt angry.

Jacob reached out to turn on the light. On the base of the lamp, a cowboy swung a lasso that formed a trimming for the bottom of the shade. The cowboy's left hand was chipped, the lasso torn. The boy who owned that lamp for the very first time would be an old man by now.

Jacob would have chosen a lamp with robots or space warriors, but like everything else he owned, the lamp was old and well-used. It made Jacob furious just to look at it.

Jacob dressed quickly and followed delicious break-fast smells coming from the kitchen. His younger brother, Peewee, was standing beside their mother at the stove.

"Can we go Christmas shopping today?" Peewee asked.

"Well, not today," Mama said.

"Not today or any day," Jacob interrupted. "Poor folks like us can't afford Christmas."

"Now Jacob . . . " Mama spoke, trying to smooth over the hurt she saw rushing into Peewee's eyes. "Maybe we won't go shopping together, but I know there's gonna be presents!"

"Sure!" said Jacob. "Maybe we'll get some old socks from that well-known clothes store, the Salvation Army!"

Jacob's bitter words mocked his mother. Hurt, she yelled back at him, "Don't you ever talk like that in this house! Ever! Do you hear me, Jacob?"

"Please don't fight!" Peewee cried. "Mama, Jacob's sorry!"

But Jacob wasn't sorry, for this scene was repeated at least once a week. The words were not always the same, but the hurt was the same. Jacob walked away and sat quietly on the same stool he always sat on. He held his head in his hands, then stared out the kitchen window, holding back his tears.

Nothing was said as Mama mixed and poured pancake batter into the skillet. Jacob knew his mother was waiting for an apology, but he couldn't speak to her.

Mama stumbled over her words. "I know it's hard on you, son. We're just going through some rough times now, but — "

Jacob broke down in a rage. "I hate being black! I hate it!"

A chill ran down Mama's back as if her spine were a huge icicle. "Being black ain't got nothing to do with it, son!"

"Everything black is bad!" Jacob repeated words he'd heard others say. "You ever hear of the Black House? No! But there's a White House. A white tornado cleans your sink; a black one destroys your house. And how about fairy tales? It's the white knight who wins, the black one who loses. Good magic is white; black magic is bad."

"That's nonsense, Jacob!" Mama answered. "Those are just tired old words I've been hearing since I was a girl!"

Peewee tugged at his mother's skirt. "Mama!"

"Not now, Peewee," Mama said, staring sadly at her older son.

Peewee tried again. "Mama!"

"Shhh," Mama said; but as she turned around, she noticed smoke rising from the pan. She looked inside and started to laugh. Peewee laughed, too.

"What's so funny?" Jacob asked.

"That is," she said. "The man in the pan."

"There's no man in there," said Jacob. "Just a black pancake."

"Child, you have no imagination." Still laughing, Mama bustled about the kitchen until her masterpiece was complete. She gave the pancake man two Cheerios for eyes and a sausage for a mouth.

Jacob tried to hold back a smile but could not. He laughed so hard he felt ready to burst. Mama tickled Jacob, then both boys tickled her back, and they all found themselves on the kitchen floor: Mama doubled over, Jacob and Peewee kicking their feet in the air.

"Do you think our pancake man is happy being black?" Jacob asked.

"Why, of course," said Mama. "Happy ain't got no color."

Then Jacob's laughter dissolved as quickly as it had come. "This is dumb," he said as he grabbed his coat and walked out the door.

The morning air was crispy cool. Patches of white snow winked brightly between puddles of gray, foot-worn slush. Horns honked at children who aimed their snowballs at buses and trucks.

Jacob stepped out into a battle. Two snowballs exploded on either side of him. He jumped out into the battlefield, dodged a few missiles, then retreated out back, where he could sit on the cellar door and be alone. But it was no use. Peewee was already on his trail.

"What do you want?" Jacob asked.

"I just want to play with my big brother," said Peewee. "Let's build a snowman."

"We can't build a snowman," Jacob snapped. "Just look at that snow. It's watery and black from all the people trampling on it."

"Then we'll make a black snowman," said Peewee.

"A black snowman," Jacob sighed. "Just what I've always wanted."

Jacob watched as Peewee packed the snow with his small hands.

"At the rate you're going, you won't be done till spring," Jacob said.

With Jacob's help, the work went quickly. The harder Jacob worked, the better he felt.

"This black snowman sure could use some dressing up," he suggested.

It was Peewee's job to pick through the trash to find a wardrobe: steel wool for hair, buttons for eyes, and a funny old hat.

Peewee looked at their snowman proudly, but Jacob had a more critical eye. "Something's missing," he said.

"Like what?" Peewee asked.

"Like it's cold out here. Find him something to wear on his shoulders."

Peewee returned to the trash, where a colorful cloth caught his eye.

"Look at this," Peewee said as he held up the cloth for his brother to see.

"Nah." Jacob scowled. "Don't use that. It doesn't go with the rest of him. Find something else."

"Well, I like it," Peewee said, "and I'm going to use it."

Peewee carefully draped the cloth around the snowman's lumpy body.

Though old and torn, the cloth began to come alive again with powers passed down through many generations. Peewee had discovered the magic *kente*.

"Now he's perfect," Peewee said.

Jacob looked at the sooty snowman in his tattered hat and shawl; he felt sad and angry at the same time.

"A black snowman," Jacob said. "Is that ugly!"

"Who are you calling ugly?"

The boys looked around but saw no one.

"Who said that?" Jacob asked.

"I did. Over here."

"It's our snowman," said Peewee, skipping with delight. "Our snowman can talk!"

Jacob stared suspiciously.

The snowman picked up Peewee and lifted him high. "Well, look here," said the snowman, "a little one who still believes."

The snowman put Peewee down again, and they danced.

"We have to go," said Jacob.

The snowman led his partner toward Jacob. "But you haven't danced yet," said the snowman. "Why, it's downright impolite not to dance with a new friend."

"You're no friend of mine," Jacob said.

The snowman walked around Jacob. He pressed his glove to Jacob's forehead and squinted his eyes in concentration.

The snowman's color changed from gray to pink; to red, yellow, blue; and finally to solid black. It was as if all the colors in space had painted themselves onto his body. He opened his eyes wide, as if he had made a sudden discovery.

"So, black is bad, huh?" said the snowman.

"That's right!" Jacob spoke up.

"What is more important in a book — the white pages, the black words, or the message the book holds?" asked the snowman.

"Huh?" Jacob looked puzzled.

"The heavens are black, and the universe is held in it," the snowman said. "Should we call the earth bad because it is cradled in blackness?"

Jacob didn't know what to say.

The snowman continued. "Have you sat at the table of your forefathers? Have you accepted the shield of courage they have passed along to you?"

Jacob hesitated. He didn't know what this crazy snowman was talking about.

"Jacob! Peewee!" Mama called from the window.

"Oh, brother, it's Mama," Peewee spoke up, then yelled back, "Coming, Ma!"

The snowman broke the spell. "We will meet again, Jacob. My work with you has just begun."

The boys scooted down the alley into the street.

In the hallway, they agreed not to tell their mother or anyone else about what had happened.

Night's curtain fell upon the day. The room was dark, except for the streetlights that showed dimly through the window.

"So what do you think about our snowman? Pretty neat, huh?" said Peewee.

"What's so neat about an ugly black snowman?" Jacob asked.

"He's no ordinary snowman," said Peewee.

"I don't want to talk about him," said Jacob.

"But he's alive!" said Peewee. "Our snowman is alive!"

"It's just in your imagination," Jacob lied. "Now go to sleep and leave me alone."

"Then let's talk about Christmas," Peewee said. "I want to get Mama something real special this year."

Jacob became angry. "Don't you understand anything? We don't have any money."

"But I have a plan. We can collect empty bottles and cans, and turn them in for refund money," Peewee explained. "If we collect a whole lot, we can buy Mama a special present. We can buy her that perfume that she likes so much. What do you think? Huh, Jacob?"

"Where are you going to get all those cans and bottles, Peewee? You'll have to walk half the city to find them."

"Oh, no," answered Peewee. "I've seen cans all over that old building across the street. That's where a lot of people throw their stuff."

"No way," said Jacob. "Don't you go near that place. The building is falling to pieces, and Mama will get angry. Anyway, I ain't looking through nobody's garbage."

Jacob could tell that Peewee was sleeping. But Jacob's mind was too crowded with confusing thoughts to fall asleep just yet.

Then Jacob heard a voice.

As Jacob approached the window, a blue-white light rose from the alley below. The snowman was standing with his hands up toward the sky. He waved at the broken wall of the building, and a single brick dislodged and fell. On its way down, the brick changed its shape, and standing in the alley was an African warrior. Then the snowman threw a trashcan lid high into the air. As it spun, it turned into a majestic black queen.

Jacob put his coat over his pajamas and ran outside.

The snowman stepped upon a mound of snow, then waved his arm and asked, "Have you studied with the scholars of Timbuktu?" Suddenly a small clump of snow transformed into a giant figure. "Or ridden with the horsemen of Bornu?" With just a wave of his arm, a horse and rider rose out of the snow. "Have you danced with the Zulu? Wrestled with the Nuba? Hunted with the Bini? Have you heard the stories of the Ashanti? The poems of the Tuareg? The prayers of the Zande?"

"Who are these people?" Jacob asked.

"They are people like you," the snowman replied. "These are strong, brave Africans from whom you descend — black people who should make you proud of your great heritage."

"I'm not like them," Jacob said. "I'm not a warrior. I'm just a boy."

Jacob ran back upstairs and hid under his blankets. But he could not fall asleep for a long, long time.

The next day, Jacob woke to see Peewee at his bedside with a shopping bag in his hand.

"This is your last chance," Peewee said. "Are you coming or not?"

Jacob rolled over, turning his back toward Peewee.

"Go hunt garbage by yourself," said Jacob, and he pretended to go back to sleep until his brother left the room.

After Jacob dressed, he poked around the kitchen stove to see what Mama was cooking for Sunday dinner.

"I'm making your favorite," said Mama.

Mama was always trying to make things better. Peewee was right. She deserved something special for Christmas.

"I'm going out for a while," Jacob said.

Jacob looked up and down the block, but Peewee was nowhere in sight.

Then SSISSBOOOMMM! An explosion.

Jacob hit the ground and hid his head. When he looked up, he saw smoke and fire coming from the abandoned building across the street.

The black snowman appeared at his side.

"Peewee is in that building," he said.

The snowman ran into the burning building with Jacob close behind.

Great licking flames devoured everything they touched. Wooden beams collapsed as the fire consumed their last bits of moisture. The air was filled with smoke — smoke that seemed to form the shapes of the great Africans — giving Jacob courage and leading him to his brother.

Jacob pressed himself close to the coolness of the snowman's body, and the snowman covered himself and the boy with the *kente*. Beneath this magical cloth, they were safe from the smoke and the flames.

In a room on the second floor, they found Peewee, huddled in a corner, sobbing between coughs, sitting next to the shopping bag that was half filled with bottles and cans.

As Jacob hugged his brother, he noticed the trail of water that the snowman was leaving behind him; the snowman's feet had melted away.

"Restore! Restore!" the snowman said, and the snow returned to his feet.

The snowman removed the *kente* from his own shoulders and wrapped the two boys in its protective magic. Under the safety of the *kente*, there was only room for two.

The snowman melted rapidly. His feet and legs had turned to slush. He walked awkwardly, bumping into burning beams and stumbling over fallen debris. His melting arms felt for the doorway and found Jacob's outstretched hand.

"Snowman," Jacob whispered.

"Restore! Restore!" the snowman repeated, but he was weakening. "Jacob, get your brother out! Jacob! Believe, Jacob. Believe in yourself. Gather up your courage. Fight, Jacob. Fight off the flames of all those bad feelings you carry inside. Believe in your strength. Believe in your love for your brother. Believe that you can save Peewee — and you will!"

Almost overcome with tears, Jacob said softly, "I believe, snowman. I believe."

"Restore!" said the snowman once again.

Jacob wrapped the cloth even more tightly around himself and his brother, and fought smoke and flames all the way down the stairs. Once again, the Africans appeared and showed Jacob the way.

When the boys reached the bottom, they turned around. The snowman was gone, leaving only a puddle of water, water that soon evaporated in the extreme heat.

"Where do you think he is?" Peewee asked.

On one of the bottom steps, Jacob noticed steel wool, buttons, and a funny old hat.

"I think he's gone," Jacob said.

As the boys left the burning building, they saw their mother break through the crowd. Jacob felt smothered in hugs and kisses. He decided that it was a good feeling.

Jacob closed his eyes and took a long, deep breath. He suddenly felt lucky to have Peewee and Mama. He felt glad to be alive and he felt good about himself. Restored — yes!

"My cans," said Peewee. "I forgot my cans for Mama's present."

"Hush," said Jacob. "We'll look for cans tomorrow. Tomorrow we'll go together."

It took several hours for the fire department to put out the blaze. Finally it was all over. On his way back to the truck, one of the firemen noticed a colorful cloth hovering over the snow. Thinking his daughter could use the cloth to make a dress for her doll, he picked it up and put it into his pocket.